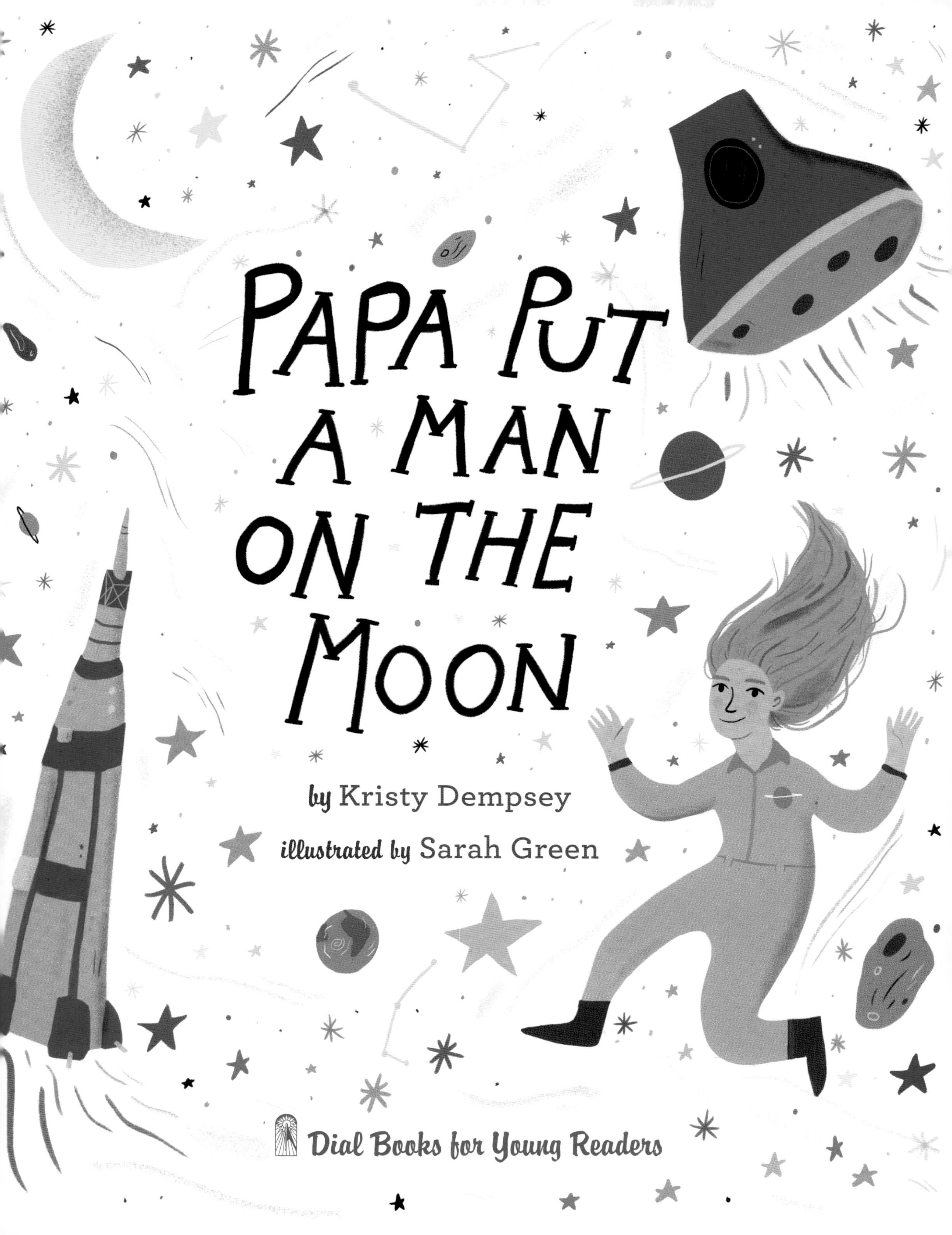
PAPA PUT A MAN ON THE MOON
by Kristy Dempsey
illustrated by Sarah Green
Dial Books for Young Readers

The full moon rises high over our hill
like a lantern shining at sea.

Papa and I sit
side by side, waiting
until that bright halo arcs
high over our heads.

When Papa points, I squint
to find the Sea of Tranquility
where the newsman Mr. Cronkite said
men will one day stand
on the surface of the moon.

I stretch my hand out straight as I can,
but the moon's too far away
to imagine an ordinary man
reaching out to touch its face,
just as easy as I touch my papa's.

Three days ago, Mama whispered to me
Papa's job at the mill changed, and now
he's doing important government work.
The fabric he weaves is one layer
in the spacesuit our astronauts wear.

I ask him,
"Papa, aren't you proud?
You work for the president!"

Papa closes his eyes and leans back on
the steps.
"Only proud to make a living, Marthanne.
Only proud to make a living."

But I know better.
We hear it on the news each night
and in chatter at the supermarket
each Saturday.

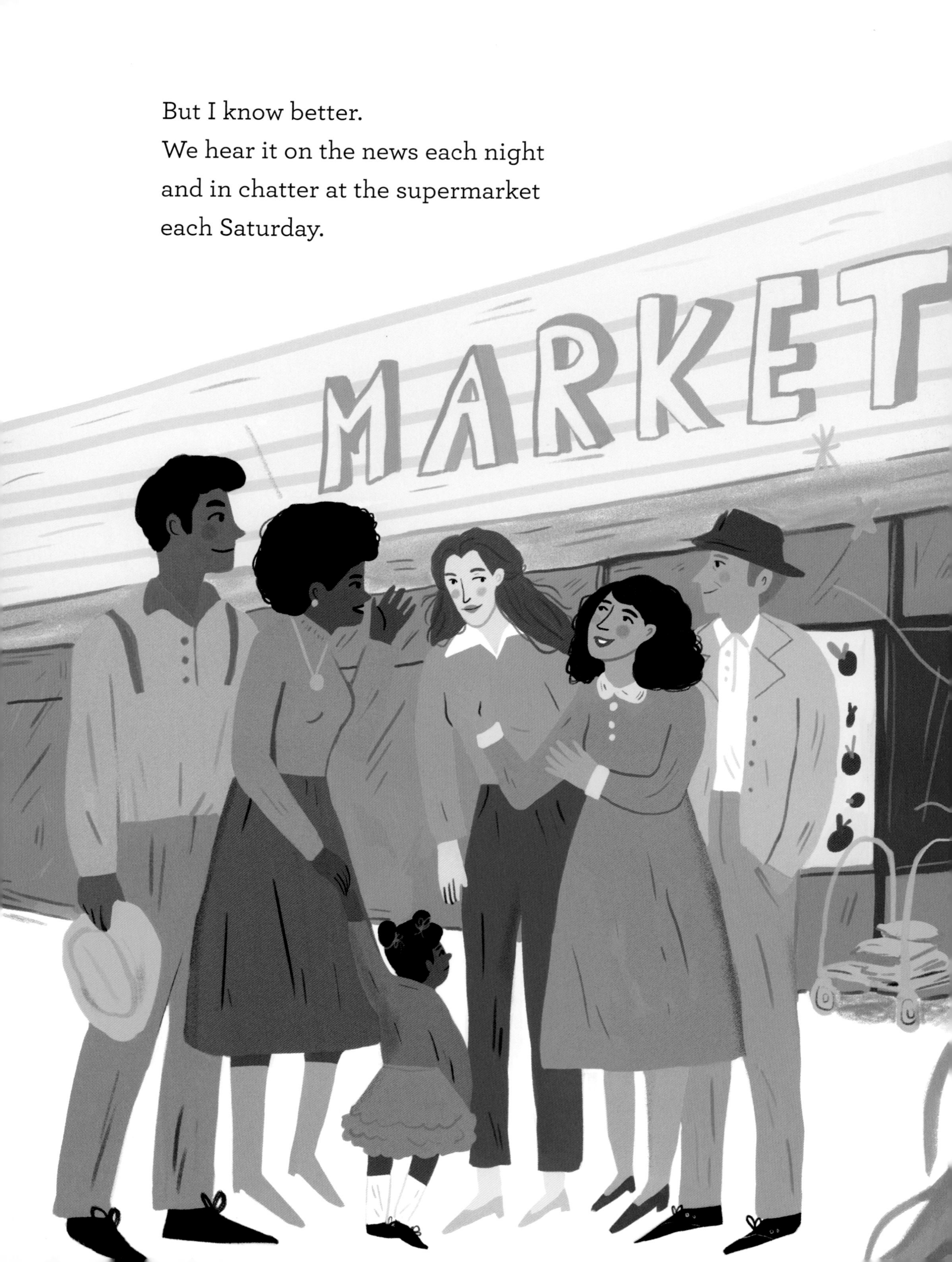

Our little mill village is one piece of something big,
bigger than we ever dared to think we could be.
I can't help but let that make me feel proud.

When it's time for bed,
Papa takes my toothbrush
and bobbles it just out of reach,
pretending it's twirling through zero gravity
like we saw the Apollo astronauts do on TV.

"To the moon!" I cry
as he snatches me up,
floating me to bed
with twists and turns.
I fall asleep dreaming I am drifting through stars.

That spring, I walk with Papa from the mill each night,
my heart heavy as blossoms on dogwood trees.
"Do you think we'll make it to the moon, Papa?"
"Nothing to do but watch and see," he says.
But time passes slowly and my hope unravels like a string.

I wish we'd hurry.

Finally,
one day come summer,
three astronauts blast off
and this time,
Mr. Cronkite says
they're going for the moon.

Watching the news,
I can practically feel
the rumble of engines
and the rush of air from the explosions
that push that rocket into the heavens.

Four days later, they're all set.
When Papa turns the TV on,
I leave my usual spot on the floor
and nestle onto the couch beside him.

Papa squishes closer to Mama
and together we listen
as the lunar module descends
toward the moon.

When Walter Cronkite takes off his glasses,
repeating,

“Oh boy, oh boy,”

my heart
starts beating
that same rhythm.

"Oh boy,

oh boy,

oh boy."

"The Eagle has landed."

Later I hold my breath
as Neil Armstrong steps from the ladder
and lands where no man has stood,
not ever before.

"One small step for man,
one giant leap for mankind."

Papa doesn't say a word
and I don't break his quiet
with what I'm thinking,
but I know it's true anyway.

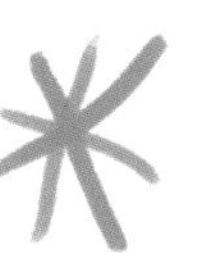

Somewhere in that spacesuit,
in the thick layers
protecting Mr. Armstrong,
are threads my Papa touched,
threads he wove together
into sheets of fabric,
the same fabric
keeping those astronauts alive
in outer space.

Those threads go from Papa—
a man whose feet have hardly left our hill—
to our astronauts,
now leaving their footprints in moon dust.

Papa says he's just making a living,
but I know better.
No need to shout it loud.
It's right there on TV
for the world to see.

My papa put a man on the moon.

AUTHOR'S NOTE

In 1962, in an effort to rally the nation around the Apollo Space Program, President John F. Kennedy declared, "We choose to go to the moon in this decade." The federal government invested billions of dollars and hired factories across the United States to build each piece of equipment needed to make this bold mission a reality. One of those factories was a J.P. Stevens textile mill in Slater, SC, where my own grandparents, parents, aunts, and uncles all worked at one time or another. In the 1960s, this mill began producing Beta cloth, a fiberglass thread fabric pioneered by Dr. Frederick Dawn, a NASA textile expert. This fabric would become one of the layers in the Apollo spacesuits. At the time, the mill workers who made this fabric felt they were simply doing their jobs, making an honest living in textiles. But when the mission was finally accomplished and Neil Armstrong stepped onto the surface of the moon, they knew they had contributed to a monumental American achievement. I wrote this book to honor the men, women, and communities across the United States that made the moon landing possible through their work ethic and dedication.

—Kristy Dempsey

To the families and children of the Slater, SC, mill hill.

—K.D.

To my father, who has always been there to support me and help make my dreams reachable. Thank you for never doubting.

—S.G.

Dial Books for Young Readers
An imprint of Penguin Random House LLC, New York

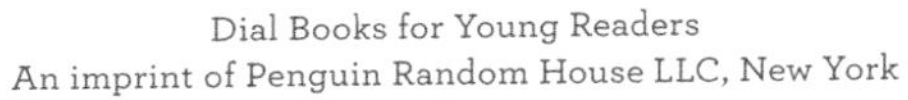

Visit us online at Penguinrandomhouse.com

Library of Congress Cataloging-in-Publication Data

Names: Dempsey, Kristy, author. | Green, Sarah, illustrator.
Title: Papa put a man on the moon / Kristy Dempsey ; illustrated by Sarah Green.
Description: New York, NY : Dial Books for Young Readers, [2019] | Summary: Marthanne's whole community is excited about the moon landing, and Marthanne is especially proud because her father helped create the fabric for the astronauts' spacesuits.
Identifiers: LCCN 2018040325 (print) | LCCN 2018053729 (ebook) | ISBN 9780525554493 (epub) | ISBN 9780525554509 (kindle) | ISBN 9780735230743 (hardback)
Subjects: | CYAC: Fathers and daughters—Fiction. | Space flight to the moon—Fiction. | BISAC: JUVENILE FICTION / Family / Parents. | JUVENILE FICTION / Historical / United States / 20th Century. | JUVENILE FICTION / Lifestyles / Country Life.
Classification: LCC PZ7.D41136 (ebook) | LCC PZ7.D41136 Pap 2019 (print) | DDC [E]—dc23
LC record available at https://lccn.loc.gov/2018040325

1 3 5 7 9 10 8 6 4 2

Design by Mina Chung • Text set in Archer • This art was created digitally.